READING CHAMPION

Spike's New House

by Damian Harvey and Ellie O'Shea

W

FRANKLIN WATTS

LONDON • SYDNEY

Meera was standing by the window with Dad.

They were waiting to see if Spike would come into the garden.

"Will he come tonight?" asked Meera.

"Maybe he will. Maybe he won't," said Dad.

It was getting dark outside.

"Look! I think I can see him,"

said Meera.

"There he is," said Dad.

"Look by your old bicycle."

"Yes!" said Meera. "I wonder

where he's going."

Dad and Meera watched

as Spike went across the grass

and around the woodpile.

The next day, Meera went outside
to play with Mum and Dad.
"We can't play," said Mum.
"It's too messy out here."
"We need to tidy up," said Dad.

"Can we make it a good garden for playing and for hedgehog visits too?" asked Meera.

"Oh yes," said Dad.

First, they gave Meera's old bicycle to a friend. Next, they put the old washing machine in the skip. "The garden looks better already," said Mum.

"This wood is no good," said Dad.

"It's rotten. It can go in the skip too."

Mum, Dad and Meera worked
all day.
At last, all that was left was
a small pile of good wood.

Then Mum saw something.

"What's that?" she said.

"Oh no! It's Spike," said Meera.

Meera was upset.

"We have broken Spike's house.

Now he has nowhere to live,"

she said.

"Don't worry," said Dad.

"We can make him a new house."

"Yes," said Mum.

"There is a good box in the shed."

They all helped to make

a new house for Spike.

Mum put it under the wood.

Meera helped carefully.

"He will like it in here," Meera said.

"Can we give him a drink of milk?"
asked Meera.

"Milk will make him sick," said Dad.
"Water is the best thing
for hedgehogs."

The next day, Meera went into
the garden to look for Spike.
Spike was not there.
"Do you think he'll use
his new house?" asked Meera.
"We will have to wait and see,"
said Dad.

After tea, Meera went to

the window to wait.

"I hope he is safe," she said.

Then, just as it was getting dark,

Meera saw something.

"It's Spike!" she cried.

"He is going into his new house.

He likes it."

"Look!" said Mum.

Meera smiled.

"I don't think Spike is

a boy hedgehog after all," she said.

Story order

Look at these 5 pictures and captions.
Put the pictures in the right order
to retell the story.

1

Spike is a mummy hedgehog!

2

Everyone clears up the wood.

3

Mum has a plan.

4

Spike visits the garden.

5

Mum and Meera spot Spike.

Independent Reading

This series is designed to provide an opportunity for your child to read on their own. These notes are written for you to help your child choose a book and to read it independently.

In school, your child's teacher will often be using reading books which have been banded to support the process of learning to read. Use the book band colour your child is reading in school to help you make a good choice. *Spike's New House* is a good choice for children reading at Orange Band in their classroom to read independently.

The aim of independent reading is to read this book with ease, so that your child enjoys the story and relates it to their own experiences.

About the book

Meera and her parents have a regular hedgehog visitor to their back garden. When they decide to have a back-garden tidy-up, they must make a new cosy home for Spike, but will he move in?

Before reading

Help your child to learn how to make good choices by asking: "Why did you choose this book? Why do you think you will enjoy it?" Look at the cover together and ask: "What do you think the story will be about?" Ask your child to think of what they already know about the story context. Then ask your child to read the title aloud. Establish that in this book, they will learn about hedgehog homes. Ask: "What do you know about hedgehogs? What habitats do they like to live in?"

Remind your child that they can sound out the letters to make a word if they get stuck.

Decide together whether your child will read the story independently or read it aloud to you.

During reading

Remind your child of what they know and what they can do independently. If reading aloud, support your child if they hesitate or ask for help by telling the word. If reading to themselves, remind your child that they can come and ask for your help if stuck.

After reading

Support comprehension by asking your child to tell you about the story. Use the story order puzzle to encourage your child to retell the story in the right sequence, in their own words. The correct sequence can be found at the bottom of the next page.

Help your child think about the messages in the book that go beyond the story and ask: "How would you care for a hedgehog if it was nesting in your garden?"

Give your child a chance to respond to the story: "Did you have a favourite part? Did you think Spike would like the new house? Why/why not?"

Extending learning

Help your child understand the story structure by using the same sentence patterning and adding different elements. "Let's make up a new story about back-garden animals. What type of animal is your story about? Where do they like to go in the garden? How can they stay safe and healthy?"

In the classroom, your child's teacher may be teaching how to read words with contractions. There are many examples in this book that you could look at with your child, for example: *it's, he'll, don't.*
Find these together and point out how the apostrophe indicates a missing letter or letters.

Franklin Watts
First published in Great Britain in 2020
by The Watts Publishing Group

Copyright © The Watts Publishing Group 2020

Series Editors: Jackie Hamley, Melanie Palmer and Grace Glendinning
Series Advisors: Dr Sue Bodman and Glen Franklin
Series Designer: Peter Scoulding

A CIP catalogue record for this book is
available from the British Library.

ISBN 978 1 4451 7082 4 (hbk)
ISBN 978 1 4451 7084 8 (pbk)
ISBN 978 1 4451 7083 1 (library ebook)

Printed in China

Franklin Watts
An imprint of
Hachette Children's Group
Part of The Watts Publishing Group
Carmelite House
50 Victoria Embankment
London EC4Y 0DZ

An Hachette UK Company
www.hachette.co.uk

www.franklinwatts.co.uk

FSC
www.fsc.org
MIX
Paper from
responsible sources
FSC® C104740

Answer to Story order: 4, 2, 5, 3, 1